HERE THEY ARE!

PROFESSOR VON VOLT IS A FAMOUSE SCIENTIST. HE DESIGNED THIS TIME MACHINE FOR THE STILTON FAMILY: THEIR MISSION IS TO DEFEAT THE PIRATE CATS AND SAVE HISTORY!

ZKII ZIIK

SPEEDRAT

UNCLE, TODAY IS *AUGUST 2.* DO YOU REMEMBER EXACTLY WHICH DAY COLUMBUS SAILED?

IF I REMEMBER CORRECTLY, HE SAILED ON AUGUST 3...

WE HAVE TO **HURRY!**

Geronimo Stilton

THE DISCOVERY OF AMERICA

PAPERCUTZ™

Geronimo Stilton

GRAPHIC NOVELS AVAILABLE FROM PAPERCUTZ™

**Graphic Novel #1
"The Discovery
of America"**

**Graphic Novel #2
"The Secret
of the Sphinx"**

**Graphic Novel #3
"The Coliseum Con"**

**Graphic Novel #4
"Following the Trail
of Marco Polo"**

**Graphic Novel #5
"The Great Ice Age"**

**Graphic Novel #6
"Who Stole The
Mona Lisa?"**

**Graphic Novel #7
"Dinosaurs in Action"**

**Graphic Novel #8
"Play It Again, Mozart!"**

**Graphic Novel #9
"The Weird Book
Machine"**

**Graphic Novel #10
"Geronimo Stilton Saves
the Olympics"**

**Graphic Novel #11
"We'll Always
Have Paris"**

**Graphic Novel #12
"The First Samurai"**

GERONIMO STILTON graphic novels are available for $9.99 each only in hardcover. Available from booksellers everywhere. You can also order online from www.papercutz.com. Or call 1-800-886-1223, Monday through Fridays, 9 – 5 EST. MC, Visa, and AmEx accepted. To order by mail, please add $4.00 for postage and handling for first book ordered, $1.00 for each additional book and make check payable to NBM Publishing. Send to: Papercutz, 160 Broadway, Suite 700, East Wing, New York, NY 10038. GERONIMO STILTON graphic novels are also available digitally wherever e-books are sold.

www.papercutz.com

Geronimo Stilton

THE DISCOVERY OF AMERICA

By Geronimo Stilton

New York

THE DISCOVERY OF AMERICA
© EDIZIONI PIEMME 2007, S.p.A.
Via Tiziano 32, 20145
Milan, Italy
Geronimo Stilton names, characters and related indicia are copyright, trademark and exclusive license of Atlantyca S.p.A
All rights reserved.
The moral right of the author has been asserted.

Text by Geronimo Stilton
Based on an original idea by Elisabetta Dami
Original cover and illustrations by LORENZO DE PRETTO
Graphics by Michela Battaglin

© 2009 – for this work in English language by Papercutz.

Original title: Geronimo Stilton Alla Scoperta Dell'America
Translation by: Nanette McGuinness

www.geronimostilton.com

Stilton is the name of a famous English cheese. It is a registered trademark of the Stilton Cheese Makers' Association.
For more information go to www.stiltoncheese.com

No part of this book may be stored, reproduced or transmitted in any form or by any means, electronic or mechanical,
including photocopying, recording, or by any information storage and retrieval system, without written permission from
the copyright holder. FOR INFORMATION PLEASE ADDRESS ATLANTYCA S.p.A.
Via Tiziano 32, 20145 Milan, Italy tel. 0039 02 43001025 - fax 0039 02 43001020.

Lettering and Production by Ortho
Michael Petranek – Associate Editor
Jim Salicrup
Editor-in-Chief

ISBN: 978-1-59707-158-1

Printed in China
August 2014 by WKT Co. LTD.
3/F Phase 1 Leader Industrial Centre
188 Texaco Road, Tsuen Wan,
N.T., Hong Kong

Distributed by Macmillan
Ninth Papercutz Printing

IT ALL STARTED ON A SCORCHING AUGUST MORNING, HERE IN NEW MOUSE CITY, THE CAPITAL OF MOUSE ISLAND. ALLOW ME TO INTRODUCE MYSELF...

THE DISCOVERY OF AMERICA

MY NAME IS STILTON, *Geronimo Stilton!* MY JOB IS TO EDIT THE RODENT'S GAZETTE, THE MOST FAMOUSE PAPER ON ALL OF MOUSE ISLAND!

WHILE MY COLLEAGUES WERE WORKING AND SWEATING AWAY, I HAD ASKED NOT TO BE *DISTURBED*; I HAD SOME IMPORTANT WORK TO GET DONE...

VERY IMPORTANT...IN FACT, ABSOLUTELY *IMPORTANT!*

SNORE SNORE

5

WHOOP! WHOOP!

MOLDY MOZZARELLA! THAT'S PROFESSOR VON VOLT'S ALARM!

WHOOP! WHOOP!

PROFESSOR VON VOLT! HOW NICE TO HEAR FROM YOU! HOW ARE YOU? YES, OF COURSE. I'M COMING...

...RIGHT NOW!

IN AN INSTANT, I RUSHED TO PROFESSOR VON VOLT'S LAB. MY BEST FRIEND HAD SOME *EXTRAORDINARY* NEWS...

HERE I AM! I RACED OVER!

THANKS, GERONIMO! I HAVE TO SHOW YOU SOMETHING...

THIS NEW INSTRUMENT INDICATES ANY CHANGE THAT CROPS UP IN THE PAST.

THIS DISPLAY LETS ME KNOW WHEN THE PIRATE CATS ARE TRAVELING THROUGH TIME TO CHANGE HISTORY TO BENEFIT THEM... AND THAT'S EXACTLY WHAT'S HAPPENING NOW!

1492

THOSE PIRATE CATS! IT'S ALWAYS THEM! WHEN THEY TRAVEL TO THE PAST THEY ALSO CHANGE THE *PRESENT*. WE'VE GOT TO STOP THEM!

GERONIMO! YOU HAVE TO CALL YOUR FAMILY...

~GULP!~ I REALLY THINK YOU'RE RIGHT!

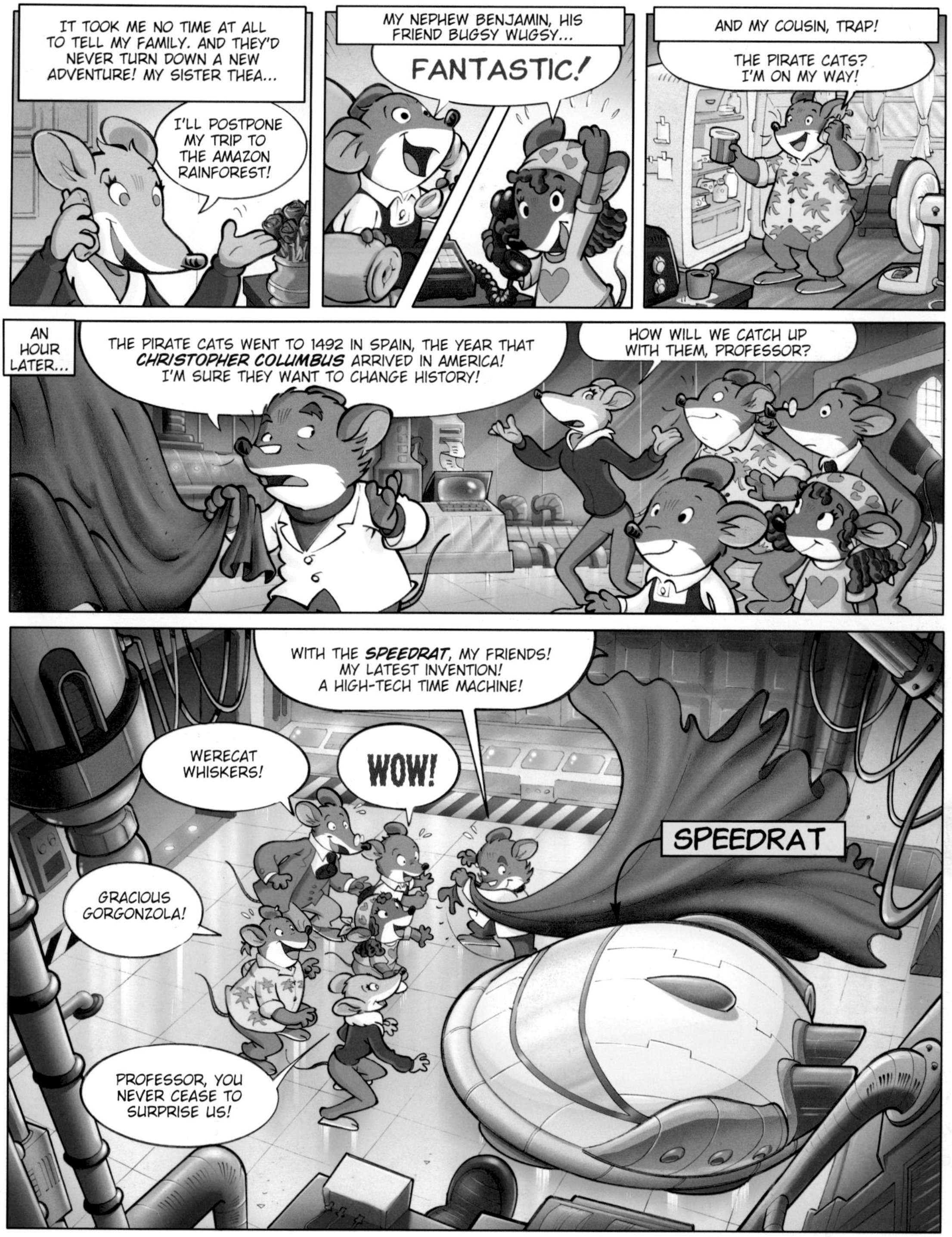
IT TOOK ME NO TIME AT ALL TO TELL MY FAMILY. AND THEY'D NEVER TURN DOWN A NEW ADVENTURE! MY SISTER THEA...
I'LL POSTPONE MY TRIP TO THE AMAZON RAINFOREST!
MY NEPHEW BENJAMIN, HIS FRIEND BUGSY WUGSY...
FANTASTIC!
AND MY COUSIN, TRAP!
THE PIRATE CATS? I'M ON MY WAY!
AN HOUR LATER...
THE PIRATE CATS WENT TO 1492 IN SPAIN, THE YEAR THAT CHRISTOPHER COLUMBUS ARRIVED IN AMERICA! I'M SURE THEY WANT TO CHANGE HISTORY!
HOW WILL WE CATCH UP WITH THEM, PROFESSOR?
WITH THE SPEEDRAT, MY FRIENDS! MY LATEST INVENTION! A HIGH-TECH TIME MACHINE!
WERECAT WHISKERS!
WOW!
SPEEDRAT
GRACIOUS GORGONZOLA!
PROFESSOR, YOU NEVER CEASE TO SURPRISE US!

HOW NICE! *ANOTHER TRIP IN TIME!* BUT...HOW WILL WE KEEP THEM FROM RECOGNIZING US?

YOU'LL FIND CLOTHING AND EVERYTHING YOU NEED FOR YOUR TRIP IN THE SPEEDRAT...

VRRRR

AND HOW WILL WE BE ABLE TO UNDERSTAND EVERYONE?

WITH THIS EARPIECE! IT'S PRACTICALLY INVISIBLE AND TRANSLATES EVERY LANGUAGE!

GREAT!

AND WHAT WILL WE EAT? MY STOMACH'S ALREADY *GROWLING--* -ACK!-

UM, PROFESSOR, DON'T LISTEN TO HIM. TELL US WHERE THE PIRATE CATS ARE INSTEAD.

...GOOD LUCK! AND REMEMBER THAT THE *FUTURE IS IN YOUR PAWS!*

IN SPAIN, IN THE CITY OF PALOS, THE PORT THAT *COLUMBUS* SAILED FROM IN THE MONTH OF AUGUST...

NEVER FEAR, PROFESSOR! WE'LL FIND THE PIRATE CATS AND STOP THEM!

AND SO WE LEFT FOR A NEW TRIP INTO TIME! WE DIDN'T KNOW WHAT DANGERS WE WOULD FACE, BUT WE KNEW WE'D BE UP TO OUR WHISKERS IN ADVENTURE!

PALOS IS A SMALL TOWN TODAY, BUT IN THE TIME OF COLUMBUS IT WAS A LARGE PORT AND IT BECAME EVEN MORE IMPORTANT DUE TO THE DISCOVERY OF AMERICA!

Spain

Palos

BACK IN PALOS IT WAS *AUGUST 1, 1492*. THE RULERS OF SPAIN, FERDINAND AND ISABELLA, HAD ASKED CHRISTOPHER COLUMBUS TO DISCOVER A NEW ROUTE TO THE INDIES, AND THE GREAT ITALIAN NAVIGATOR WAS GETTING READY TO DEPART...

CALAMITOUS CATS! NOW WHERE WILL WE PUT THE *CATJET*?

IN THE MEANTIME, THE PIRATE CATS HAD ARRIVED IN PALOS AND WERE GETTING READY FOR THEIR MISSION...

NO ONE MUST FIND OUR *TIME MACHINE!* LET'S COVER IT UP WITH SOME OF THAT TRASH.

CATJET

HOP TO IT, HAIRBALL!

THOSE OVERFED BALLS OF FUR! I ALWAYS HAVE TO DO THE WORST JOBS!

NOW THAT WE'RE IN SPAIN, WHAT WILL WE DO? ARE WE GOING TO GO RIGHT TO THE PORT?

YEAH, *TERSILLA!* WHAT ARE WE GOING TO DO? ARE WE GOING TO GO TO SEE *REAL MADRID* PLAY?

DON'T MOUSE OFF,* BONZO! *SOCCER* HASN'T BEEN INVENTED YET!

LET'S PUT ON OUR MOUSE MASKS NOW... THEN WE CAN GET DRESSED AT THE COAST...

I HAVE TO LOOK LIKE A SAILOR, TOO!

MOUSE EARS

MOUSE NOSE

*DON'T TALK NONSENSE!

9

LATER, AT THE PORT...

THE PIRATE CATS WITH THEIR MOUSE MASKS ON!

LISTEN, RODENTS! I'M MINESTRONE MOUSTRONI, *THE ROYAL INSPECTOR!* I SPEAK IN THE NAME OF THE KING. WE NEED EXPERT SAILORS WHO ARE STRONG AND FEARLESS...

THE ROYAL INSPECTOR TRAVELED WITH COLUMBUS. HE WAS IN CHARGE OF REPORTING EVERY DETAIL OF THE MISSION TO KING FERDINAND AND QUEEN ISABELLA.

YOU SURE LOOK FUNNY IN THAT MOUSE MASK!

HOW DARE YOU! I'M YOUR **BOSS!**

MEOW DOWN!* DO YOU WANT THEM TO DISCOVER US!?

NEXT!

*CALM DOWN!

AND WHAT CAN YOU DO?

I'VE SERVED THREE KINGS, SAILED EVERY SEA, DISCOVERED HUNDREDS OF TREASURES AND AM AN EXPERT HELMSMAN...

SAILOR, IF HALF OF WHAT YOU SAY IS TRUE, YOU'RE JUST THE RODENT FOR US...

MY COMPANIONS AND I WOULD BE HAPPY TO SERVE UNDER THE GREAT COLUMBUS!

WHAT COMPANIONS? **THOSE TWO OVER THERE?**

HEY, DUMMY! YOU THINK YOU'RE A BETTER SAILOR THAN ME? WHO SAYS SO?

MY MAMA SAYS SO!

!!!

WE NEED A GOOD HELMSMAN, BUT WE DON'T WANT ANY ROUGH-NECKS. GO TELL THEM TO KNOCK IT OFF...THEN *FOLLOW ME!*

THIS IS THE **SANTA MARIA**, THE FLAGSHIP OF THE GREAT CHRISTOPHER COLUMBUS. THE OTHER TWO SHIPS ARE THE **NINA** AND THE **PINTA**.

MAGNIFICENT SHIPS, SIR! WITH THEM, WE CAN BRAVE ANY KIND OF **SEA!**

CAPTAIN! HERE ARE AN **EXPERT HELMSMAN** AND TWO **DECK HANDS** FOR YOU!

HMM... LET'S SEE WHO YOU BROUGHT ME!

MY GOOD RODENTS! DO YOU KNOW WHERE WE'RE GOING?

SURE! WE'RE GOING TO AM-- →ACK!←

NO, CAPTAIN! WE DON'T KNOW!

WE'RE SAILING TO THE **INDIES!** BUT WE'RE SAILING WEST! SO WE'RE GOING TO SHOW THAT THE EARTH IS **ROUND!**

THE INDIES, DURING THE TIME OF COLUMBUS, AMERICA'S EXISTENCE WASN'T YET KNOWN. COLUMBUS'S PLAN WAS TO KEEP SAILING WEST TO REACH THE INDIES!

CAPTAIN COLUMBUS! WE DON'T UNDER-STAND!

SUFFERING SQUEAKERS! YOU DON'T HAVE TO UNDERSTAND! YOU'RE JUST DECK HANDS!

CAN YOU TACKLE A JOURNEY THIS LONG AND **DANGEROUS?**

OF COURSE, CAPTAIN! UNDER YOUR LEADERSHIP, I'LL GUIDE THIS SHIP TO THE ENDS OF THE EARTH!

COLUMBUS SHOWS THE NEW HELMSMAN HIS SHIP...

HERE'S THE TILLER! FROM HERE YOU CAN GUIDE THE SHIP. AND IF YOU DO YOUR WORK WELL, I'LL REWARD YOU PROPERLY...

I WON'T DISAPPOINT YOU!

11

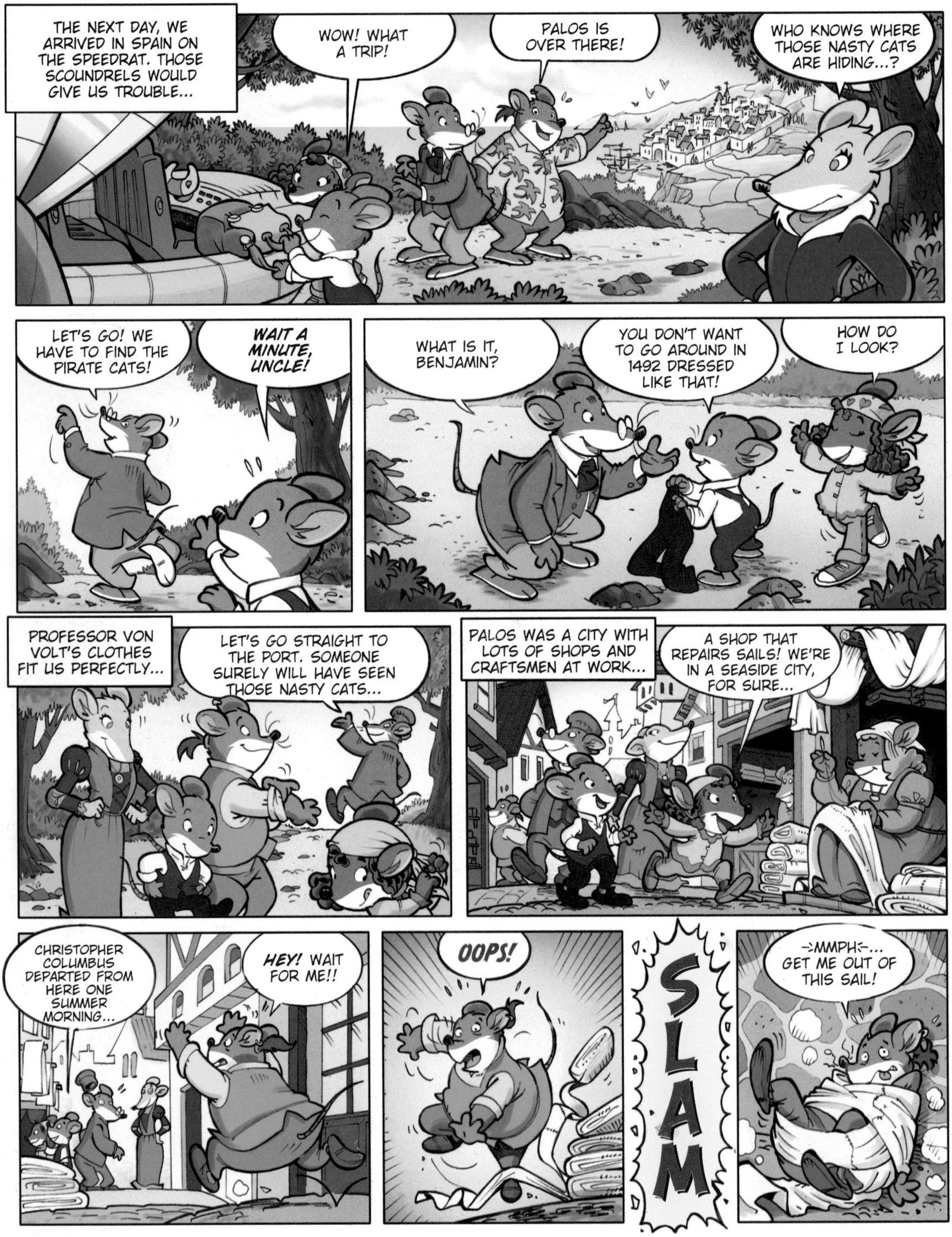
THE NEXT DAY, WE ARRIVED IN SPAIN ON THE SPEEDRAT. THOSE SCOUNDRELS WOULD GIVE US TROUBLE...
WOW! WHAT A TRIP!
PALOS IS OVER THERE!
WHO KNOWS WHERE THOSE NASTY CATS ARE HIDING...?
LET'S GO! WE HAVE TO FIND THE PIRATE CATS!
WAIT A MINUTE, UNCLE!
WHAT IS IT, BENJAMIN?
YOU DON'T WANT TO GO AROUND IN 1492 DRESSED LIKE THAT!
HOW DO I LOOK?
PROFESSOR VON VOLT'S CLOTHES FIT US PERFECTLY...
LET'S GO STRAIGHT TO THE PORT. SOMEONE SURELY WILL HAVE SEEN THOSE NASTY CATS...
PALOS WAS A CITY WITH LOTS OF SHOPS AND CRAFTSMEN AT WORK...
A SHOP THAT REPAIRS SAILS! WE'RE IN A SEASIDE CITY, FOR SURE...
CHRISTOPHER COLUMBUS DEPARTED FROM HERE ONE SUMMER MORNING...
HEY! WAIT FOR ME!!
OOPS!
SLAM
MMPH... GET ME OUT OF THIS SAIL!

UNCLE, TODAY IS *AUGUST 2*. DO YOU REMEMBER EXACTLY WHICH DAY COLUMBUS SAILED?

IF I REMEMBER CORRECTLY, HE SAILED ON AUGUST 3...

WE HAVE TO **HURRY!**

SHORTLY THEREAFTER WE ARRIVED AT THE AREA AROUND THE PORT. I WAS SURE THE CATS WOULDN'T BE TOO FAR AWAY...

WHAT CHEERFUL PEOPLE! SHALL WE GO IN AND HAVE SOMETHING TO *eat?*

OH, HOW NICE TO SAIL AWAY, ON EVERY SEA AND EVERY DAY!

posada

HEY LOOK!

WHAT DID YOU SEE?

LOOK AT THIS PILE OF TRASH...

WHAT IS IT ABOUT THIS THAT DOESN'T FIT?

BACK THEN, CITY-DWELLERS DIDN'T COLLECT THEIR TRASH; THEY THREW IT INTO THE STREET...

...BUT THEY'VE THROWN OUT SOME VERY STRANGE TRASH FROM THIS INN...

WHO COULD HAVE EATEN ALL THESE *FISH?*

WHAT A HORRIBLE **SMELL!**

FISH? HMM...

HEY! MOLDY MOZZARELLA!

SPLASH

WHAT ARE YOU DOING THERE?

WATCH WHAT YOU'RE DOING, YOU CLUMSY IDIOT!

EXCUSE US, BUT... WHAT KIND OF A RODENT CAN EAT SO MUCH FISH?

I THOUGHT IT WAS STRANGE THAT THOSE STRANGERS ASKED FOR FISH, TOO... USUALLY MICE LIKE CHEESE!

"I OFFERED THEM MY BEST DISHES, BUT THOSE GUYS DIDN'T WANT TO TASTE ANY OF THEM..."

NO! NO SOUP, NO CHEESE! WE WANT FISH!

YES, LOTS OF FISH! GILTHEAD, SEA BASS, AND WHITEFISH!

AND WHERE WERE THESE STRANGERS HEADED?

THEY WERE SAILORS AND WANTED TO GO TO SEA. THEY ASKED ME WHICH WAY THE PORT WAS...

THEY WERE LOOKING FOR COLUMBUS'S SHIPS... HEY! DON'T YOU WANT TO EAT SOMETHING?

COME ON! LET'S GET TO THE PORT!

TEN MINUTES LATER...

HERE'S THE PORT!

WHAT BEAUTIFUL SHIPS!

BUT HOW ARE WE GOING TO FIND THE PIRATE CATS?

≈PANT, PANT≈ DO YOU KNOW WHERE COLUMBUS'S SHIPS ARE?

COLUMBUS? THAT WEIRD GUY?

OVER THERE YOU'LL FIND OTHER *FOOLS* LIKE YOU WHO WANT TO GO TO SEA WITH THAT DREAMER!

WE FINALLY GOT TO COLUMBUS'S SHIPS...

HERE THEY ARE!

COME FORWARD! THE CREW IS ALMOST COMPLETE!

THESE ARE COLUMBUS'S SAILORS! THE CATS CAN'T BE FAR OFF!

HEY! WAIT FOR ME!

OOPS!

OW!

MEOW!!!

LOOK WHERE YOU PUT YOUR PAWS, TAIL SMASHER!

SORRY, MISTER!

LITTLE MOUSELINGS SHOULD STAY HOME!

HE HURT YOU, EH? HA! HA!

HMM...

WHEN BENJAMIN FELL ON HIS TAIL, THAT SAILOR SAID *MEOW!*

MEOW?

NO! HE SAID CIAO!

SHUT UP! HE SAID WOW!

BUT HE SAID... BOW-WOW!

BOW-WOW? WHAT'S THAT? A NEW CURSE WORD?

I'M SURE IT WAS *MEOW!*

MEOW, EH? HMM...

THOSE TWO ARE PART OF CAPTAIN COLUMBUS'S CREW...

ARE YOU THINKING WHAT I'M THINKING, GERONIMO?

ALAS, YES, KID SISTER!

WHAT DO YOU THINK... OF A LITTLE OCEAN JOURNEY?

YESSSS!

HEY! JUST A MINUTE!

I DON'T KNOW ANYTHING ABOUT SAILING!

LUCKILY I'M HERE. I KNOW HOW TO DO EVERYTHING!

EVERY-THING?

GO ON, ANSWER! I'M *MINESTRONE MOUSARONI*, THE REPRESENTATIVE FOR SPAIN. AND THIS IS *MACARONI MOUSARONI*, MY WIFE!

I CAN DO MANY TRADES... I KNOW HOW TO TELL *JOKES*, DANCE, MAKE MUSIC...

AND... DO YOU KNOW HOW TO *COOK*?

YES... YES... WHY?

AND YOU, DO YOU KNOW HOW TO STYLE A LADY'S HAIR?

OF COURSE!

GOOD! WRITE IT DOWN: THIS ONE'S BOARDING! HE'LL BE THE *COOK*!

AND THIS YOUNG LADY WILL BE MY TRAVELING COMPANION...

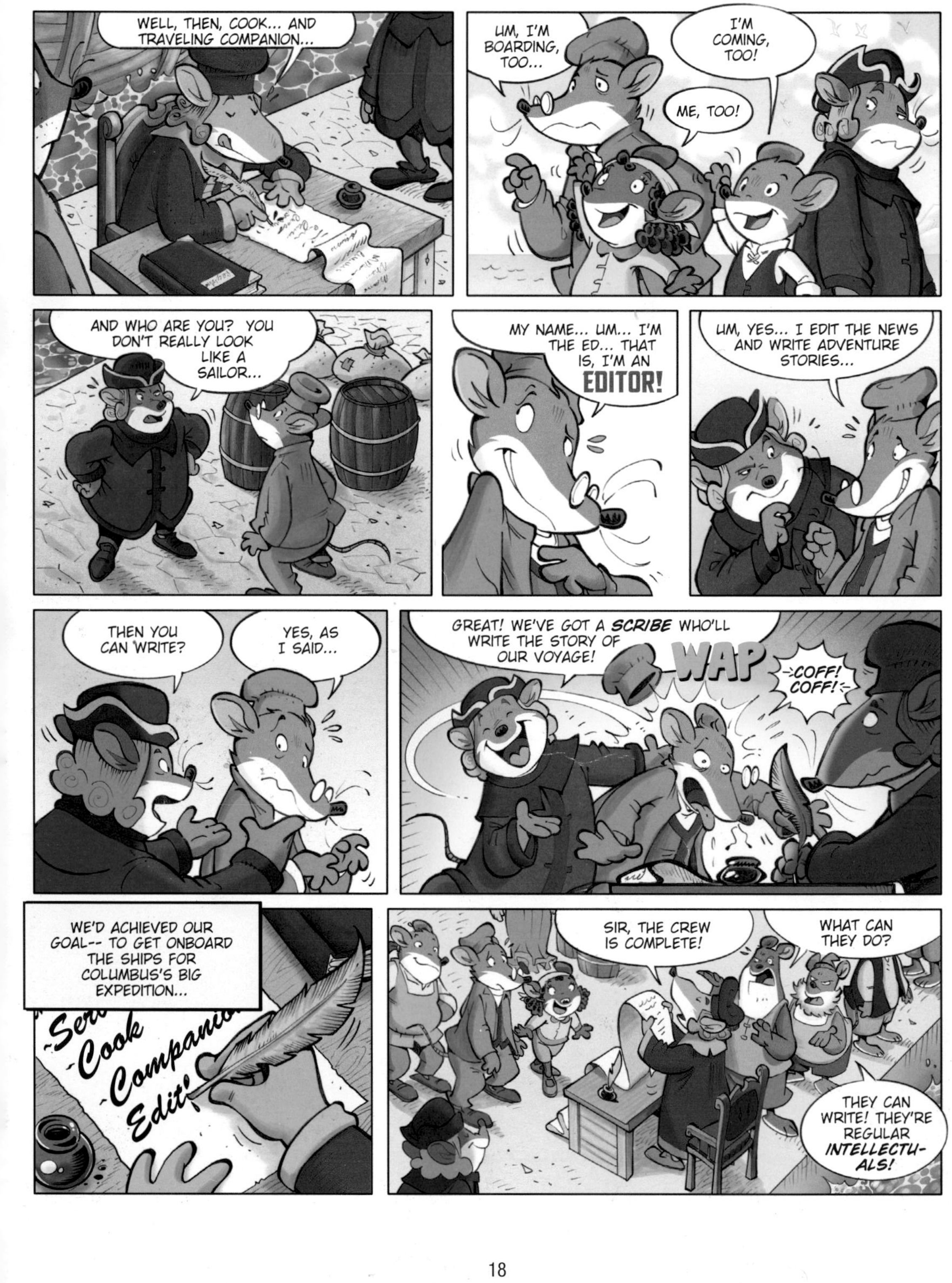
WELL, THEN, COOK... AND TRAVELING COMPANION...
UM, I'M BOARDING, TOO...
I'M COMING, TOO!
ME, TOO!
AND WHO ARE YOU? YOU DON'T REALLY LOOK LIKE A SAILOR...
MY NAME... UM... I'M THE ED... THAT IS, I'M AN EDITOR!
UM, YES... I EDIT THE NEWS AND WRITE ADVENTURE STORIES...
THEN YOU CAN WRITE?
YES, AS I SAID...
GREAT! WE'VE GOT A SCRIBE WHO'LL WRITE THE STORY OF OUR VOYAGE!
WAP
COFF! COFF!
WE'D ACHIEVED OUR GOAL-- TO GET ONBOARD THE SHIPS FOR COLUMBUS'S BIG EXPEDITION...
SIR, THE CREW IS COMPLETE!
WHAT CAN THEY DO?
THEY CAN WRITE! THEY'RE REGULAR INTELLECTU-ALS!

AUGUST 3, 1492, WAS A BIG DAY FOR PALOS. THE WHOLE CITY CAME TO THE PORT TO CELEBRATE COLUMBUS'S DEPARTURE...

GOODBYE, PALOS!

CIAO!

WE'RE OFF!

SQUEEEAK!

BYE! BYE, EVERYONE!

I HOPE I DON'T GET SEASICK!

EVERYONE AGREES! WE'LL SHTEAL COMMAND OF THE SHIP...

BUT SOMEBODY HAD SOMETHING ELSE IN MIND...

IT'S PRONOUNCED STEAL... AND WE'LL STEAL IT WHEN I SAY SO!

HA! HA!

ARE WE REALLY GOING TO FIND THE INDIES, CAPTAIN?

CERTAINLY! I'VE BEEN PREPARING FOR THIS EXPEDITION FOR YEARS!

IT TOOK COLUMBUS NEARLY TEN YEARS TO FIND SPONSORS FOR HIS EXPEDITION. AS A MATTER OF FACT, HE HAD ALREADY PRESENTED HIS PROJECT IN 1483 TO THE KING OF PORTUGAL.

WE'LL FOLLOW THIS COURSE FOR TWO WEEKS. THEN, WE'LL HEAD SOUTH. THEN FINALLY WE'LL HEAD WESTWARD AGAIN. THE INDIES AREN'T FAR!

DID YOU WRITE THAT DOWN, SCRIBE? KING FERDINAND WANTS A FAITHFUL CHRONICLE OF THE TRIP.

OF COURSE! WHEN THE KING READS MY CHRONICLE, IT'LL BE AS IF HE HAD TRAVELED WITH US!

IT WILL BE A MAGNIFICENT ACHIEVEMENT!

LET'S HOPE SO!

From the scribe's chronicle.
"THE SAILORS AREN'T AFRAID OF ANYTHING..."

BRRR! THIS 'FRAIDY CAT'S SCARED!

"THE COOK NEVER STOPS WORKING, EVEN WHEN FACED WITH THE HARDEST TASKS..."

‑SOB! SOB!‑ I HATE ONIONS!

"EXPERT SAILORS STEER OUR SHIPS."

WUMP

OUCH! PAY ATTENTION, YOU IDIOT!

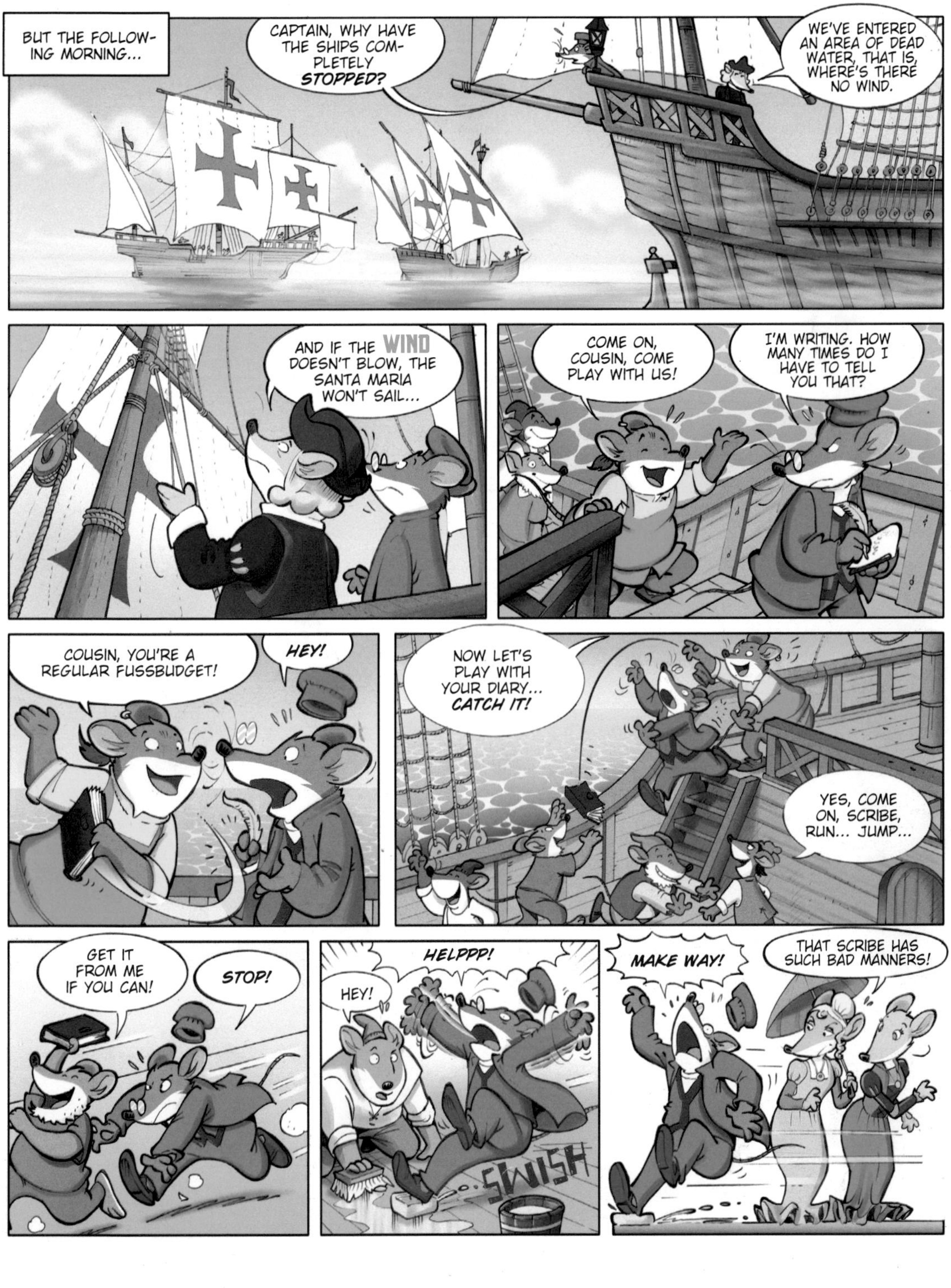
BUT THE FOLLOWING MORNING...
CAPTAIN, WHY HAVE THE SHIPS COMPLETELY **STOPPED?**
WE'VE ENTERED AN AREA OF DEAD WATER, THAT IS, WHERE'S THERE NO WIND.
AND IF THE WIND DOESN'T BLOW, THE SANTA MARIA WON'T SAIL...
COME ON, COUSIN, COME PLAY WITH US!
I'M WRITING. HOW MANY TIMES DO I HAVE TO TELL YOU THAT?
COUSIN, YOU'RE A REGULAR FUSSBUDGET!
HEY!
NOW LET'S PLAY WITH YOUR DIARY... **CATCH IT!**
YES, COME ON, SCRIBE, RUN... JUMP...
GET IT FROM ME IF YOU CAN!
STOP!
HELPPP!
HEY!
SWISH
MAKE WAY!
THAT SCRIBE HAS SUCH BAD MANNERS!

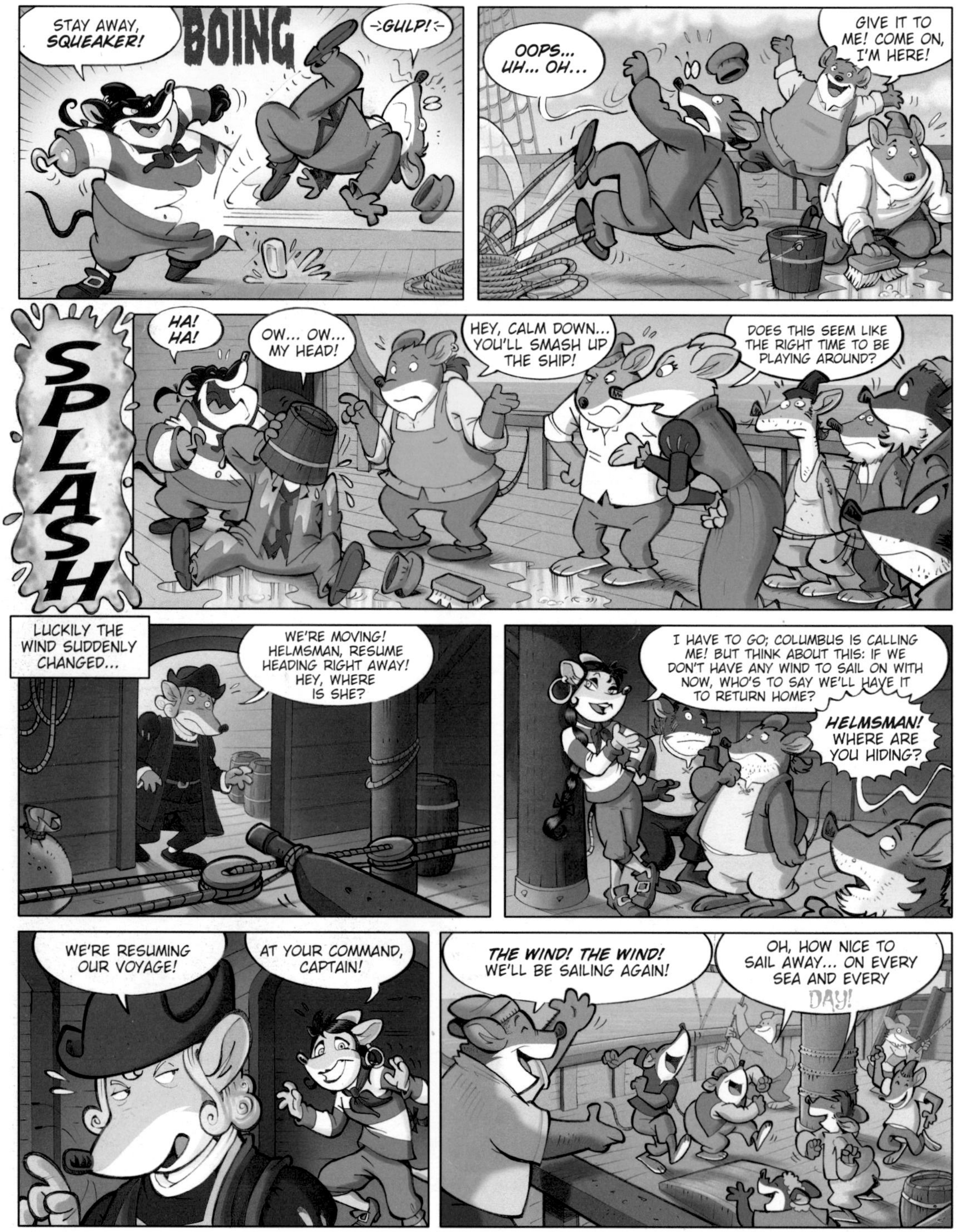
STAY AWAY, SQUEAKER!
BOING
GULP!
OOPS... UH... OH...
GIVE IT TO ME! COME ON, I'M HERE!
SPLASH
HA! HA!
OW... OW... MY HEAD!
HEY, CALM DOWN... YOU'LL SMASH UP THE SHIP!
DOES THIS SEEM LIKE THE RIGHT TIME TO BE PLAYING AROUND?
LUCKILY THE WIND SUDDENLY CHANGED...
WE'RE MOVING! HELMSMAN, RESUME HEADING RIGHT AWAY! HEY, WHERE IS SHE?
I HAVE TO GO; COLUMBUS IS CALLING ME! BUT THINK ABOUT THIS: IF WE DON'T HAVE ANY WIND TO SAIL ON WITH NOW, WHO'S TO SAY WE'LL HAVE IT TO RETURN HOME?
HELMSMAN! WHERE ARE YOU HIDING?
WE'RE RESUMING OUR VOYAGE!
AT YOUR COMMAND, CAPTAIN!
THE WIND! THE WIND! WE'LL BE SAILING AGAIN!
OH, HOW NICE TO SAIL AWAY... ON EVERY SEA AND EVERY DAY!

A FEW DAYS LATER...

...YOU'VE GOT TO BELIEVE ME, MY TWO COUSINS, SAILORS FROM SEVILLE...

...WERE SAILING TOWARDS THE WEST, A FEW MILES OFF THE COAST OF AFRICA...

OF COURSE! I REMEMBER THEM... WHAT HAPPENED TO THEM IN THE END?

I'M NOT SURE IT'S A GOOD IDEA TO TELL YOU ABOUT IT. MY WHISKERS ARE QUIVERING WITH FEAR...

BE BRAVE! TELL US ABOUT IT! WE'RE NOT AFRAID OF ANYTHING!

ONE OF THEM NEVER CAME HOME AGAIN. AND DO YOU KNOW WHY? A HORRIBLE SEA MONSTER SPRANG UP OUT OF THE WATER...

...IT FOLLOWED THEM FOR DAYS! IT HAD TWO HEADS AND EIGHT TENTA-CLES WITH HOOKS AT THE ENDS, AND A MOUTH THAT SPOUTED FLAMES...

BUT IF IT FOLLOWED THEM FOR DAYS, WHY DIDN'T THEY RACE AWAY FROM IT FIRST?

AT THE START, THE ONLY SIGN IT WAS THERE WAS A TERRIBLE STENCH..

THE NEXT MORNING, STRANGELY ENOUGH...

WHAT A **SMELL!** WHAT'S GOING ON?

THAT COULDN'T BE, BY ANY CHANCE...

...THE SMELL OF THE MONSTER!

UNCLE! UNCLE! WHERE IS THAT STENCH COMING FROM? IS IT REALLY THE SMELL OF THE MONSTER?

MONSTER? WHO'S BEEN TALKING ABOUT **MONSTERS?** BRRR, THIS 'FRAIDY CAT'S SCARED!

THE MONSTER!

~BLECH~ WHAT A STINK!

THE SMELL IS COMING FROM DOWN THERE! LET'S GO CHECK IT OUT...

BUT MAYBE...

WE HAVE TO FIND WHERE THAT SMELL COMES FROM!

IT SURE IS DARK HERE! YOU CAN'T EVEN MAKE OUT A MORSEL OF MOZZARELLA!

HERE'S WHERE THE REPAIR SUPPLIES ARE STORED...

AND... THE STENCH IS QUITE STRONG... DO YOU WANT TO... GO ON?

WHAT'S IN THESE BARRELS, UNCLE?

UM... *SAND...* TO MAKE THE SHIP STABLE...

HERE ARE THE SUPPLIES!

LET'S GET AWAY FROM HERE... WE COULD CHOKE!

WHAT A SMELL!

UNCLE! THE SMELL IS COMING FROM THIS CHEST!

WHERE? EVERYONE STOP! LET'S INFORM CAPTAIN COLUMBUS!

ON DECK, A FEW MINUTES LATER...

THUD

OPEN IT!

THE SMELL OF THE MONSTER!

THE MONSTER'S IN THE CHEST!

-UGH!-

WE SHOULDN'T HAVE OPENED IT!

-BLEH!-

-GULP!-

BLUB

MOLDY MOZZARELLA! IT'S ROTTEN FISH!

WHAAAT?!

WHO PLAYED THIS JOKE? IF I FIND THEM, I'LL MAKE THEM EAT MUSSELS FOR A MONTH...

THUD

...BETTER YET, WE'LL ABANDON THEM ON A DESERT ISLAND!

THERE'S NOTHING BETTER THAN ROTTEN FISH TO MAKE SOMEONE BELIEVE THEY'VE SMELLED A MONSTER!

A FEW HOURS HAD PASSED WHEN...

HELP!!!

HELP! HELPPP! HURRY!

WHAT'S GOING ON?

A MONSTER!

WHY ARE YOU CALLING FOR HELP?

I SAW A MONSTER!

A MONSTER! HE SAYS HE SAW A MONSTER!

THEN IT'S TRUE! WHERE THERE'S A STENCH, THERE'S A MONSTER!

WHERE DID YOU SEE IT?

IN THE SEA! IT WAS HUGE! IT HAD TWO HEADS AND EIGHT TENTACLES!

I SAW IT! I SAW IT! ME, TOO!

IT WAS ENORMOUS! IT HAD THREE HEADS AND SIX TENTACLES... NO, RATHER, IT HAD FOUR HEADS AND TWO TENTACLES...

A SEA MONSTER!

OUR LIVES ARE IN DANGER!

WE'LL BECOME CAT KIBBLE!

WHAT IS ALL THIS RACKET?

CAPTAIN, WE SPOTTED A MONSTER!

A HUGE MONSTER WITH THREE HEADS AND FIVE TENTACLES!

NO! WITH TWO HEADS AND EIGHT HOOKED TENTACLES!

SEA MONSTERS DON'T EXIST! DON'T BELIEVE THAT SUPERSTITIOUS NONSENSE!

BUT, CAPTAIN...

SILENCE! STOP WASTING TIME AND GET BACK TO WORK!

IT HAD TWO HEADS AND EIGHT TENTACLES!

NO! WE SAID THREE HEADS AND SIX TENTACLES!

TWO HEADS!

THREE HEADS!

BRAINLESS CATS!

A LITTLE LATER...

THE PAW PRINTS OF THE PIRATE CATS ARE ALL OVER THAT MONSTER STORY, I'M SURE OF IT...

YES, BIG BROTHER, IT'S TIME TO INVESTIGATE SERIOUSLY!

WHY DID I EVER LEAVE HOME? WHY? WHY? WHY?

WE BEGAN GOING AROUND ASKING QUESTIONS...

UM... IS EVERYTHING OKAY?

STEER CLEAR, SCRIBE, AND LET US PLAY IN PEACE!

SCRAM, CHEESEHEAD!

WHO DIDN'T EAT THESE CHEESE SOUFFLES?

ODD THAT THERE'S SOMEBODY ON BOARD WHO DOESN'T LIKE CHEESE...

THE SANTA MARIA'S MAST IS THE TALLEST IN THE FLEET!

UM, EXCUSE ME...

GOOD THING WE DON'T GET VERTIGO!

HEY! YOU ONLY FALL FROM HERE ONCE...

-GULP!-

LOOKIE, LOOKIE AT WHAT'S OVER HERE!

ONLY CATS CAN LEAVE THESE SCRATCHES!

28

WE EVEN SEARCHED AT NIGHT...

~ZZZZ... ROAR... GRUNT...~

WHAT CAN I DO ABOUT THIS?

SNORE

SNORE

FINALLY WE GOT TOGETHER TO COMPARE NOTES...

I SPENT A SLEEPLESS NIGHT, BUT I DIDN'T DISCOVER ANYTHING!

I FOUND SOME SIGNS...

I FOUND THREE PLATES OF CHEESE SOUFFLE THAT WEREN'T EATEN AND THREE CAT SCRATCHES ON THE MAST! DOESN'T THAT TELL YOU SOMETHING?

NO RODENT HAS EVER LEFT ANY OF MY CHEESE SOUFFLE!

THIS ALL CONFIRMS THAT THE CATS ARE REALLY HERE ON THE SANTA MARIA...

THOSE CATS' DAYS ARE NUMBERED...

OUCH! LOOK OUT!

ZAK

AND YOU? DID YOU FIND ANYTHING OUT? NO ONE PAYS ANY ATTENTION TO MOUSELINGS LIKE YOU...

ACTUALLY, UNCLE, WE DID NOTICE SOMETHING...

THE SAILORS WHO SCARED THE CREW WITH THOSE STORIES AND TOLD ABOUT THE STINK ARE THE SAME ONES WHO SAID THEY SAW THE MONSTER...

THIS COINCIDENCE ISN'T AN ACCIDENT... WHAT IF THEY'RE THE PIRATE CATS DRESSED AS MICE?

THEN WE SHOULD KEEP OUR EYES OPEN! BUT WATCH OUT! IT COULD BE DANGEROUS...

-ARGH!-

WHAP

CALAMITOUS CATS, IT'S TRUE! WE HAVE TO BE CAREFUL!

ACTUALLY, LIFE ONBOARD WAS VERY DANGEROUS...

OW!

BONK

OOPS! SORRY! HEE! HEE! HEE!

HA, HA, HA,

OUCH!

OOPS!

SPLASH

WATCH OUT, SCRIBE! WE'RE WORKING ON THE SHIP HERE!

-GLUB!- -SPIT!-

BUT WE DIDN'T YET REALIZE THAT ALL THIS WAS PART OF THE PIRATE CATS' PLAN!

HA! HA!

YOU SHOULD HAVE SEEN THAT RODENT SPITTING! HA! HA!

HEY! I'VE GOT AN IDEA! WHY NOT FIX THAT SCRIBE ONCE AND FOR ALL?

RIGHT! ONLY HE CAN PREVENT US FROM *SHTEALING* THE SHIP...

REALLY, IT'S PRONOUNCED *STEAL*... BUT LET'S THINK ABOUT THE SCRIBE LATER... REMEMBER THE PLAN: GET THE SAILORS TO MUTINY, TAKE COMMAND OF THE SHIP IN PLACE OF COLUMBUS, DISCOVER AMERICA OURSELVES AND BECOME RICH!

GOOD! SO FAR WE'VE JUST BEEN FOOLING AROUND! NOW LET'S GET SERIOUS!

A FEW DAYS LATER WE WERE HIT BY A RAGING STORM...

CREW BELOW DECKS! ONLY THE RIGGING CREW ON DECK!

WHY DID I EVER LEAVE HOME? WHY? WHY?

YOU! GET TO THE CROW'S NEST AND DON'T LOSE SIGHT OF THE NINA AND THE PINTA!

~GULP!~

BELOW DECK AND CROW'S NEST THE FIRST TERM REFERS TO THE AREA UNDER A SHIP'S DECK, UNDER COVER. THE CROW'S NEST, ON THE OTHER HAND, IS A WOODEN PLATFORM AT THE TOP OF A SHIP'S MAST.

UM... CAN'T I GO BELOW DECK, TOO?

GET UP TO THE CROW'S NEST!

AND SO...

I NEVER SHOULD'VE LEFT HOME!

THE CARGO! WE'RE LOSING THE CARGO!

I NEVER SHOULD'VE LEFT HOME!

MOUSE... ALMOST OVERBOARD!!

I NEVER SHOULD'VE LEFT HOME!

KRA-KRAK

CAPTAIN COLUMBUS! WE'VE LOST THE FORESAIL!

IMPOSSIBLE! WHAT'S GOING ON WITH MY SHIP!

I NEVER SHOULD'VE LEFT HOME!

MASTS
COLUMBUS'S SHIPS HAD THREE MASTS: IN THE CENTER WAS THE MAINMAST, IN THE PROW (THAT IS, IN THE FRONT) WAS THE FOREMAST AND IN THE STERN (THAT IS, IN THE BACK OF THE SHIP), THE MIZZENMAST.

THE MORNING AFTER THE STORM HAD FINALLY PASSED THROUGH...

DID THE STORM DO A LOT OF DAMAGE, CAPTAIN?

IT'S NO LAUGHING MATTER! BUT EVERYTHING CAN BE REPAIRED...

...EXCEPT FOR THE FORESAIL! THE SAILORS SAY IT WAS HIT BY A GUST OF WIND STRONGER THAN THE REST. BUT LUCKILY WE HAVE A SPARE...

-:PSST!:- -:PSST!:-
UNCLE!

WE'VE DISCOVERED SOMETHING *TERRIBLE!*

YES, UNCLE, WE DISCOVERED WHY THE SAIL BLEW AWAY! LOOK!

SEE? IT WASN'T THE WIND: THE LINE THAT HELD THE SAIL *WAS CUT, JUST LIKE THAT!*

YOU'RE RIGHT, KIDS! AND I THINK I KNOW WHO DID IT...

ARE YOU THINKING WHAT WE'RE THINKING?

YES... THIS HAS THE PAW PRINTS OF THE PIRATE CATS! BUT WHERE COULD THEY BE HIDING THEMSELVES?

THE JOURNEY CONTINUED PEACEFULLY FOR A FEW DAYS, UNTIL...

NOW WE HAVE THE WIND AT OUR BACKS AND WE'LL TRAVEL FASTER THAN EVER!

GOOD, CAPTAIN! I'M LOOKING FORWARD TO REACHING THE INDIES!

WE'LL HAVE A LOT TO TALK ABOUT WHEN WE RETURN!

INDEED, MY FRIENDS WILL BE SO JEALOUS!

~BLEAH!~

~GLUB!~ THIS WATER IS *SAAAAAAALTED!*

MINE, TOO!

YUCK! SALTWATER? *THAT'S IMPOSSIBLE!*

CAPTAIN! WE GAVE THE SAILORS SALTWATER!

IT WOULDN'T BE ONE OF YOUR USUAL PRANKS?

I ONLY PLAY JOKES ON YOU! I DON'T KNOW WHAT COULD HAVE HAPPENED!

34

MUTINY BROKE OUT AMONG THE CREW NOW...

IT'S TRUE! WE CAN'T TAKE IT ANY MORE!

ENOUGH ALREADY! TOO MUCH HAS HAPPENED!

ROTTEN ROQUEFORT! THIS TRIP SHOULD NEVER HAVE HAPPENED!

LET'S DEMAND THAT THE CAPTAIN...

WHAT?

WHAT DO YOU WANT TO DEMAND OF THE CAPTAIN?

TO GO BACK HOME!

YES, LET'S GO HOME!

HOME! ENOUGH WITH OCEANS! LONG LIVE BATHTUBS!

RODENTS THIS VALIANT WHO WANT TO GO BACK?

THIS TRIP IS IMPOSSIBLE!

I'VE NEVER SEEN ANYTHING LIKE IT...

YES, WE'RE BEING COMMANDED BY A CHARLATAN!

STOP WASTING YOUR BREATH! WHO DOESN'T HAVE PROBLEMS AT SEA?

MANY OF YOU HAVE SAILED WITH ME BEFORE AND KNOW I ALWAYS KEEP MY PROMISES!

WE'VE ALREADY FIGURED OUT WHAT HAPPENED WITH THE WATER...

ONE OF THE BARRELS IS FULL OF SALTWATER, BUT THE OTHERS ALL HAVE THE BEST WATER THERE IS...

LISTEN TO THE COOK! IT'S A MATTER OF A SIMPLE MISTAKE WHEN WE DEPARTED. SO...

...EVERYONE GET TO WORK!

IS THAT TRUE? THAT STORY DOESN'T CONVINCE ME...

ONE MORE THING AND I'M SWIMMING BACK HOME...

MMM... WHO COULD'VE LOADED SALTWATER ONBOARD? AND WHAT ELSE CAN STILL HAPPEN?

THAT NIGHT, THE WHOLE CREW SLEPT ON THE DECK DUE TO THE HEAT...

-ZZZZ-
-ZZZZ-

-ZZZZ-

Z

I WAS DREAMING ABOUT DELICIOUS CHOCOLATE AND GORGONZOLA, WHEN..

ZZZ MEOW
ZZZ
MEOW

-SNORE-
MEOW
ZZZ

MOLDY MOZZARELLA! I'LL NEVER GET TO SLEEP HERE! AND THAT SAILOR...

...SAID ...MEOW! A CAT! I'M SCARED OF CATS!

-SNORE...
MEOWWW...
ZZZZ...
MEOWWW...-

-ZZZ...- UGLY RODENT FACE... MEOW... WE'LL TAKE COMMAND OF THE SHIP OURSELVES... -ZZZ...-

BRRR, HOW SCARY! BUT I'VE GOT TO BE BRAVE AND DISCOVER THESE SCOUNDRELS' PLANS!

-ZZZZ- ... WE'LL BRING THE SHIPS TO AMERICA... -ZZZ-... WE'LL GET VERY RICH... MEOW...

!!!

MEOW... THE KING OF SPAIN WILL NAME US VICEROY... -SNORE-... ALL THE CATS IN AMERICA WILL BE ACKNOWLEDGED... -ZZZZZZ-...

THOSE COMMON CROOKS!

HOW WILL YOU DO THIS?

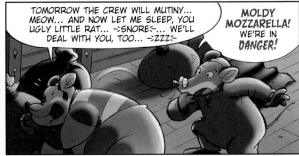

TOMORROW THE CREW WILL MUTINY... MEOW... AND NOW LET ME SLEEP, YOU UGLY LITTLE RAT... →SNORE←... WE'LL DEAL WITH YOU, TOO... →ZZZ←

MOLDY MOZZARELLA! WE'RE IN DANGER!

A FEW MINUTES LATER...

NOW YOU KNOW EVERYTHING I KNOW. WHAT SHOULD WE DO?

WE'LL BLOW THE WHISTLE ON THEM TO CAPTAIN COLUMBUS...

HE'LL NEVER BELIEVE OUR STORY...

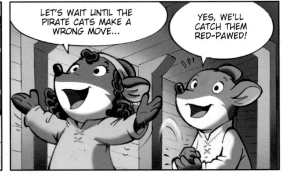

LET'S WAIT UNTIL THE PIRATE CATS MAKE A WRONG MOVE...

YES, WE'LL CATCH THEM RED-PAWED!

THAT'S RIGHT, GERONIMO! WE'VE GOT TO UNMASK THEM RIGHT AS THEY SWING INTO ACTION!

HMM... ARE YOU SURE? WON'T IT BE... DANGEROUS?

LIGHTEN UP, COUSIN! I'LL HELP YOU SAVE HISTORY!

→AKK!← THAT'S RIGHT! EVEN THAT MUST HAVE HAPPENED TO ME, TOO!

THE NEXT DAY, COLUMBUS THREW A PARTY...

YOU DANCE DIVINELY! AND YOU'RE AS LIGHT AS A FEATHER!

THANK YOU, SIR!

YOU DANCE LIKE A TRUE GENTLEMOUSE, SCRIBE!

YOU'RE MAKING ME BLUSH... UM.. MA'AM...

ATTENTION! ACCORDING TO MY CALCULATIONS, WE'RE MORE THAN HALFWAY THROUGH OUR VOYAGE! TO *CELEBRATE*, THERE'S AN EXTRA RATION OF CHEESE FOR EVERYONE!

COME ON, COOK! DOUBLE RATIONS FOR EVERYONE!

I'M GOING... AND I'LL BE RIGHT BACK!

HURRAH! HURRAH!

MEALS
THE ONLY HOT MEAL OF THE DAY WAS AT 11 O'CLOCK. IN THE EVENING, COLD RATIONS OF CRACKERS AND A LITTLE DRIED MEAT AND CHEESE WERE DISTRIBUTED.

BUT IT LOOKED LIKE A HURRICANE HAD COME THROUGH THE SHIP. IN FACT, IN THE KITCHEN...

!!??

CALAMITOUS CATS! THE CHEESE IS ALL GONE? JUST YESTERDAY THERE WAS PLENTY OF IT...

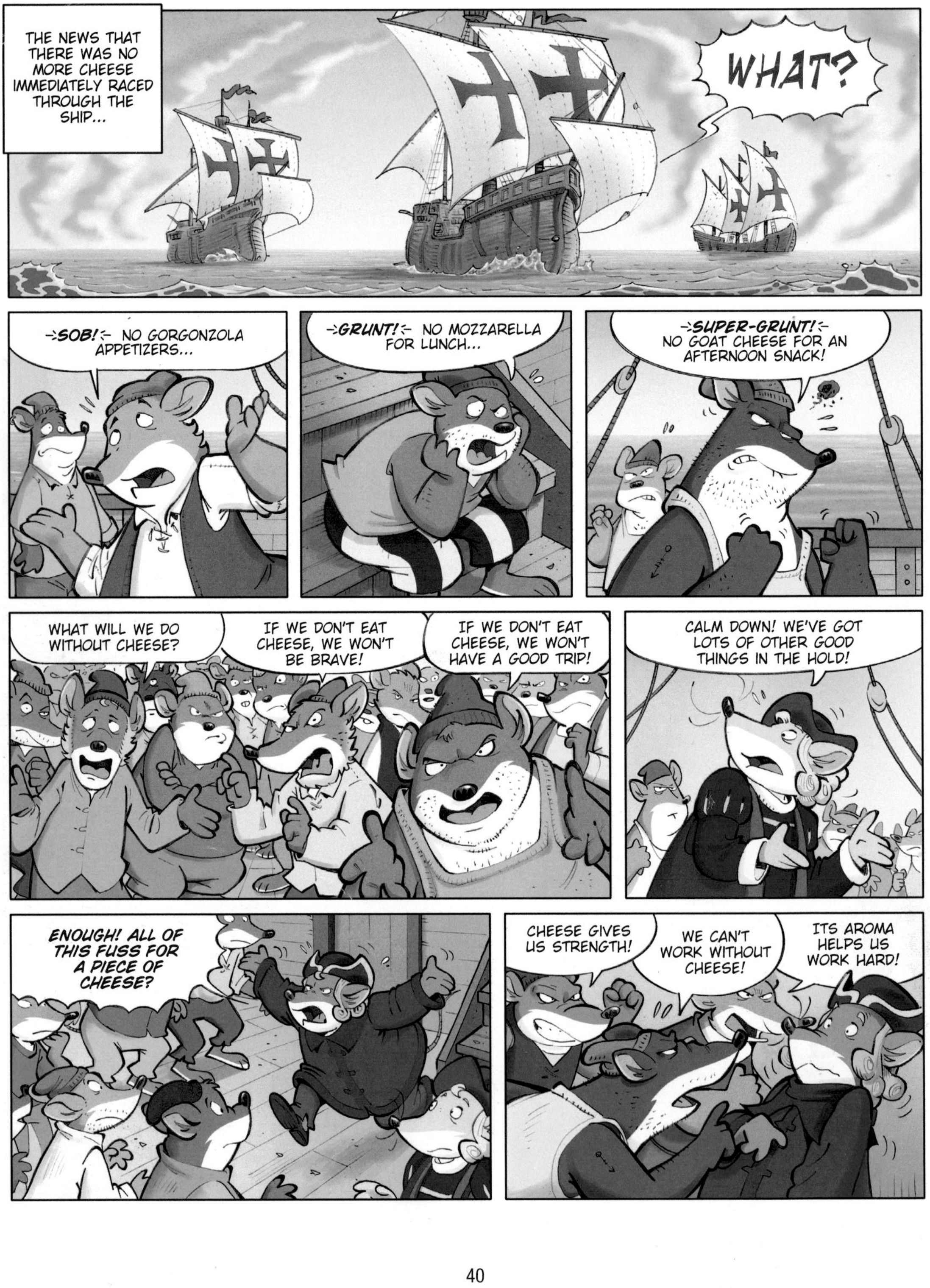
THE NEWS THAT THERE WAS NO MORE CHEESE IMMEDIATELY RACED THROUGH THE SHIP...
WHAT?
SOB! NO GORGONZOLA APPETIZERS...
GRUNT! NO MOZZARELLA FOR LUNCH...
SUPER-GRUNT! NO GOAT CHEESE FOR AN AFTERNOON SNACK!
WHAT WILL WE DO WITHOUT CHEESE?
IF WE DON'T EAT CHEESE, WE WON'T BE BRAVE!
IF WE DON'T EAT CHEESE, WE WON'T HAVE A GOOD TRIP!
CALM DOWN! WE'VE GOT LOTS OF OTHER GOOD THINGS IN THE HOLD!
ENOUGH! ALL OF THIS FUSS FOR A PIECE OF CHEESE?
CHEESE GIVES US STRENGTH!
WE CAN'T WORK WITHOUT CHEESE!
ITS AROMA HELPS US WORK HARD!

?!?

ENOUGH ALREADY!

!?!

SAILORS! DO WE HAVE TO KEEP PUTTING UP WITH ALL THIS?

WHAT DO YOU MEAN, HELMSMAN?

YES, EXPLAIN!

LET'S TAKE COMMAND OF THE EXPEDITION!

WE CAN EAT ALL WE WANT AND NO ONE WILL GIVE US ANY MORE ORDERS...

BY THE FLEA-RIDDEN FUR OF A WERECAT! WHAT AN IDEA!

GO ON! WE'RE LISTENING!

THINK! HOW MANY PROBLEMS HAVE WE HAD ON THIS VOYAGE?

TAKE MY ADVICE! WE'LL GET THERE SOONER IF WE'RE IN COMMAND OF THE SANTA MARIA!

THE HELMSMAN IS RIGHT! I WANT TO EAT!

ME, TOO!

WE DON'T EVEN KNOW WHERE WE'RE GOING...

WE'RE GOING TO THE INDIES! AND I PROMISE EVERYONE WILL BECOME RICH AND FAMOUS!

DON'T BELIEVE CAPTAIN COLUMBUS! ASK HIM WHAT HE'S GOING TO DO WITH THE TREASURE FROM THE INDIES?

WE'RE SAILING UNDER THE ORDERS OF THE KING... IT'LL BE UP TO HIM TO DECIDE!

AND WHAT WILL BE LEFT FOR US? THE CRUMBS, RIGHT?

SPLASH

!!!

HEE HEE...

WATER?

BE BRAVE, COUSIN! THIS IS OUR MOMENT!

BUT... BUT...

IT REALLY IS...

..WATER!!!

MEOWWWW! I CAN'T STAND WATER!

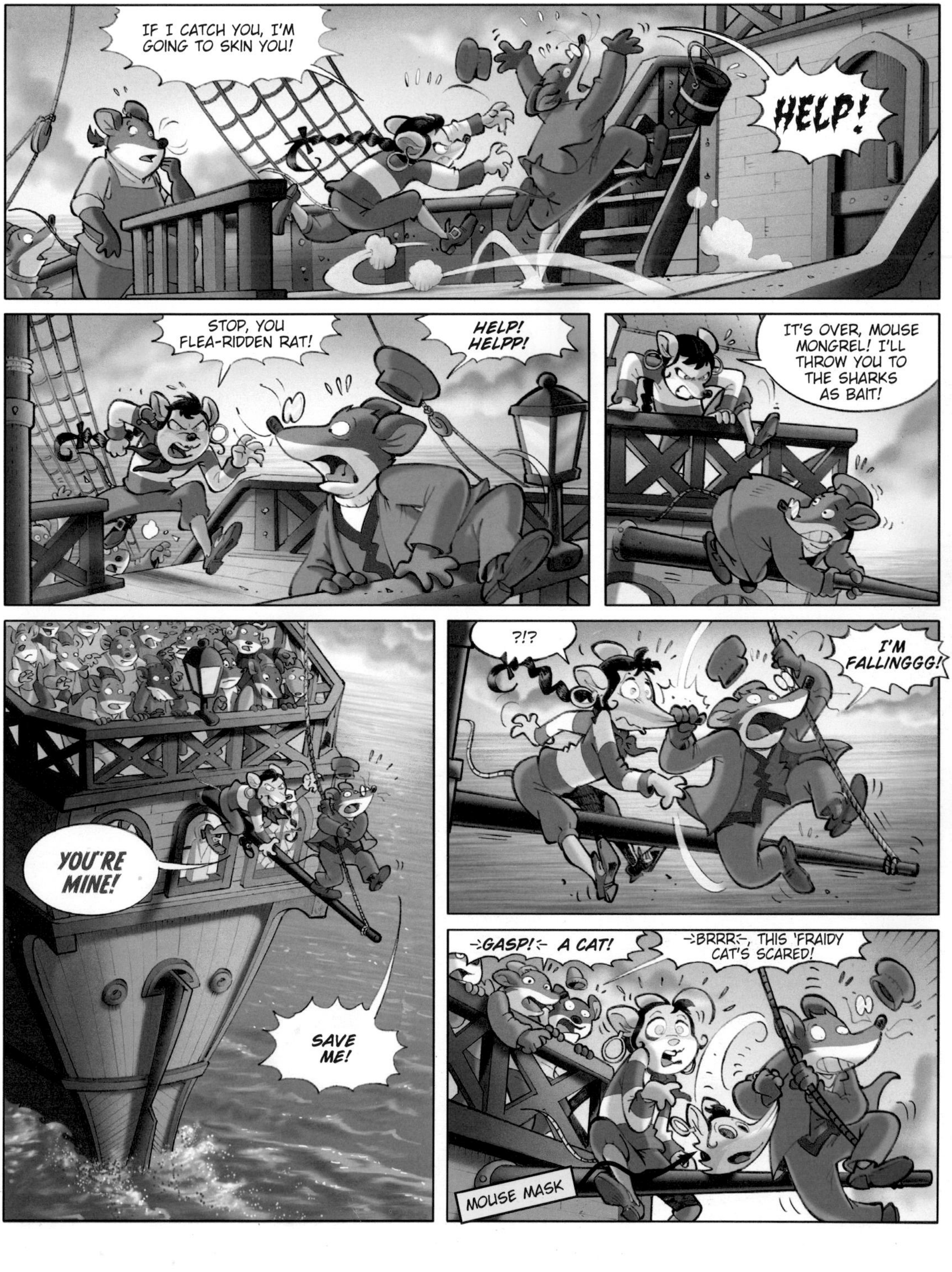
IF I CATCH YOU, I'M GOING TO SKIN YOU!
HELP!
STOP, YOU FLEA-RIDDEN RAT!
HELP! HELPP!
IT'S OVER, MOUSE MONGREL! I'LL THROW YOU TO THE SHARKS AS BAIT!
YOU'RE MINE!
SAVE ME!
?!?
I'M FALLINGGG!
-GASP!- A CAT!
-BRRR-, THIS 'FRAIDY CAT'S SCARED!
MOUSE MASK

THIS CAT IS TERSILLA, THE DAUGHTER OF...

...CATARDONE, RULER OF THE PIRATE CATS!

AND THIS IS HIS ACCOMPLICE, BONZO CAT!

WE FINALLY UNMASKED THEM...

...AND WE SAVED HISTORY!

A LITTLE LATER...

I DON'T NOW HOW TO THANK YOU, SCRIBE. YOU SAVED MY MISSION!

THEY WANTED TO TAKE CONTROL OF THE SHIP BUT THEY DIDN'T SUCCEED!

NOW THAT EVERYTHING'S WORKED OUT, START THE PARTY UP AGAIN! LET'S GET DANCING!

AT YOUR ORDERS, CAPTAIN!

TAKE THESE SCOUNDRELS AWAY! WE'LL DECIDE WHAT TO DO WITH THEM LATER...

>GRRR!<

CAPTAIN COLUMBUS, I HAVE AN IDEA!

THE VOYAGE CONTINUED PEACEFULLY...

...OR JUST ABOUT!

OOPS!

MY MAP!

SPLAT

I WROTE DOWN THE STORY, TOGETHER WITH THAT MOUSE..

AND IT WAS THANKS TO ME THAT THE PIRATE CATS WERE CAPTURED...

MACARONI MOUSARONI CHOSE THE OUTFIT SHE WAS GOING TO WEAR FOR DISEMBARKING WHEN WE ARRIVED AT THE INDIES...

WHICH LOOKS BETTER ON ME, THE YELLOW OR THE RED?

BENJAMIN AND BUGSY WUGSY HAD FUN WITH THE REST OF THE CREW...

OH, HOW GOOD TO SAIL AWAY ON EVERY SEA AND EVERY DAY!

IN SHORT, EVERYONE WAS HAPPY...

I'M TELLING YOU! WE HAVE A REALLY GREAT CAPTAIN!

...WHILE THE PIRATE CATS PAID FOR THEIR MISTAKES!

IT WAS ALL YOUR FAULT!

NO! IT WAS ALL YOUR FAULT!

IT WAS ALL YOUR FAULTS!

FINALLY ONE MORNING...

OH, HOW I WISH I WERE IN NEW MOUSE CITY!

NO MORE OCEAN ADVENTURES! I'M A QUIET GUY, OR RATHER, A QUIET MOUSE...

BUT THAT... THAT IS...

LAND!

AMER--!

WHAT AM I SAYING? I MUSTN'T CHANGE THE COURSE OF HISTORY!

LAND! LAND HO! LAND HO!

WITHIN A FEW SECONDS, THE WHOLE CREW WAS CLIMBING ONTO THE DECK, ECHOING MY CRIES!

LAND!

MOLDY MOZZARELLA! I SEE IT, TOO!

IT'S REALLY LAND!

YES! IT'S LAND! I WAS RIGHT! WE REACHED THE INDIES!

SAN SALVADOR COLUMBUS HAD NOT REACHED THE INDIES. THE LAND HE SAW ON OCTOBER 12, 1492, WHICH HE NAMED SAN SALVADOR, WAS AN ISLAND IN THE BAHAMAS, IN AMERICA.

I CLAIM THIS LAND ON BEHALF OF MY SOVEREIGN, THE GREAT KING OF SPAIN, FERDINAND OF CASTILE...

...AND QUEEN ISABELLA OF ARAGON...

CAPTAIN, UM...

...WE HAVE VISITORS...

!!!

WHAT'S YOUR NAME?

!?!

✱ MY FAMILY AND I BID YOU WELCOME, STRANGER!

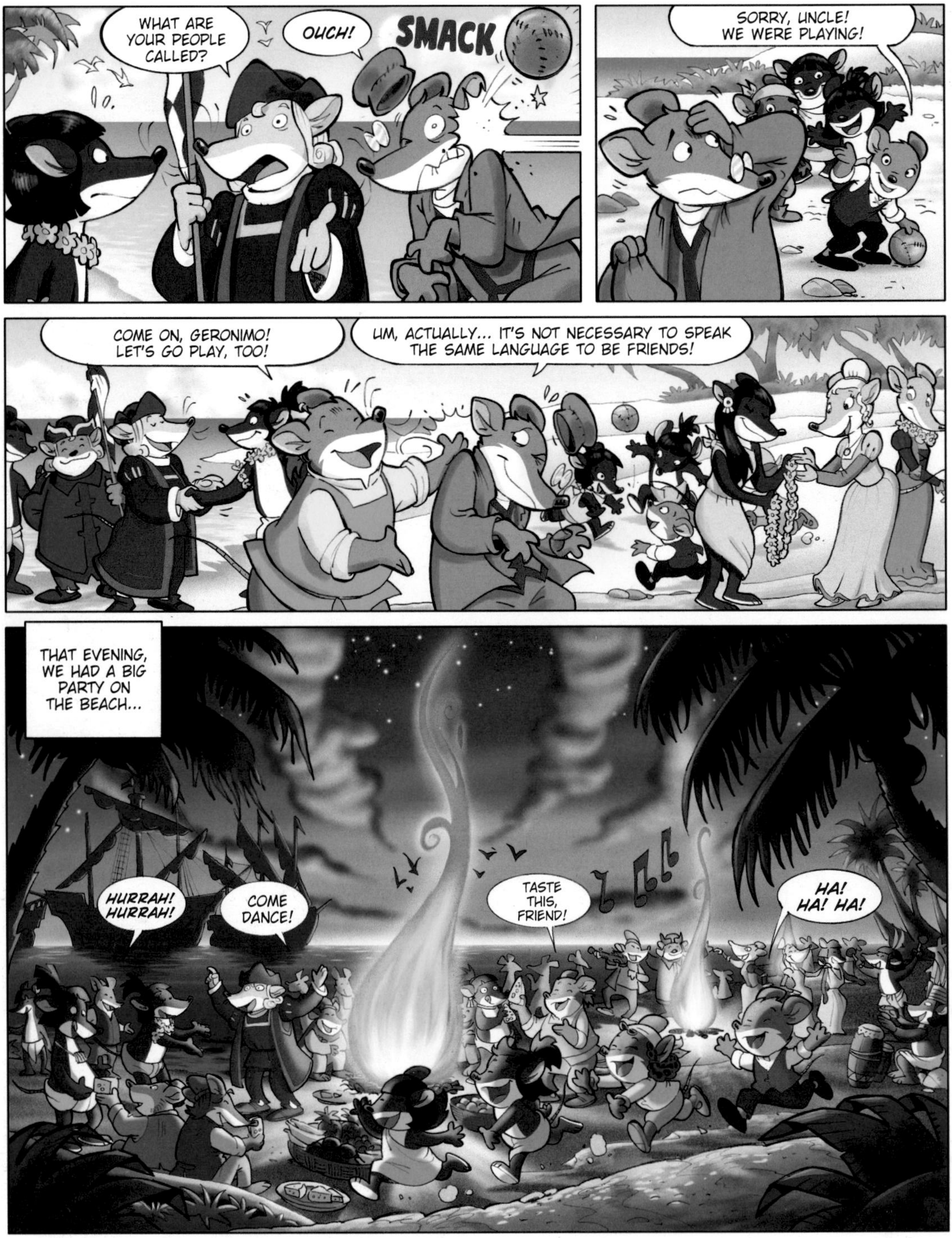
WHAT ARE YOUR PEOPLE CALLED?
OUCH!
SMACK
SORRY, UNCLE! WE WERE PLAYING!
COME ON, GERONIMO! LET'S GO PLAY, TOO!
UM, ACTUALLY... IT'S NOT NECESSARY TO SPEAK THE SAME LANGUAGE TO BE FRIENDS!
THAT EVENING, WE HAD A BIG PARTY ON THE BEACH...
HURRAH! HURRAH!
COME DANCE!
TASTE THIS, FRIEND!
HA! HA! HA!

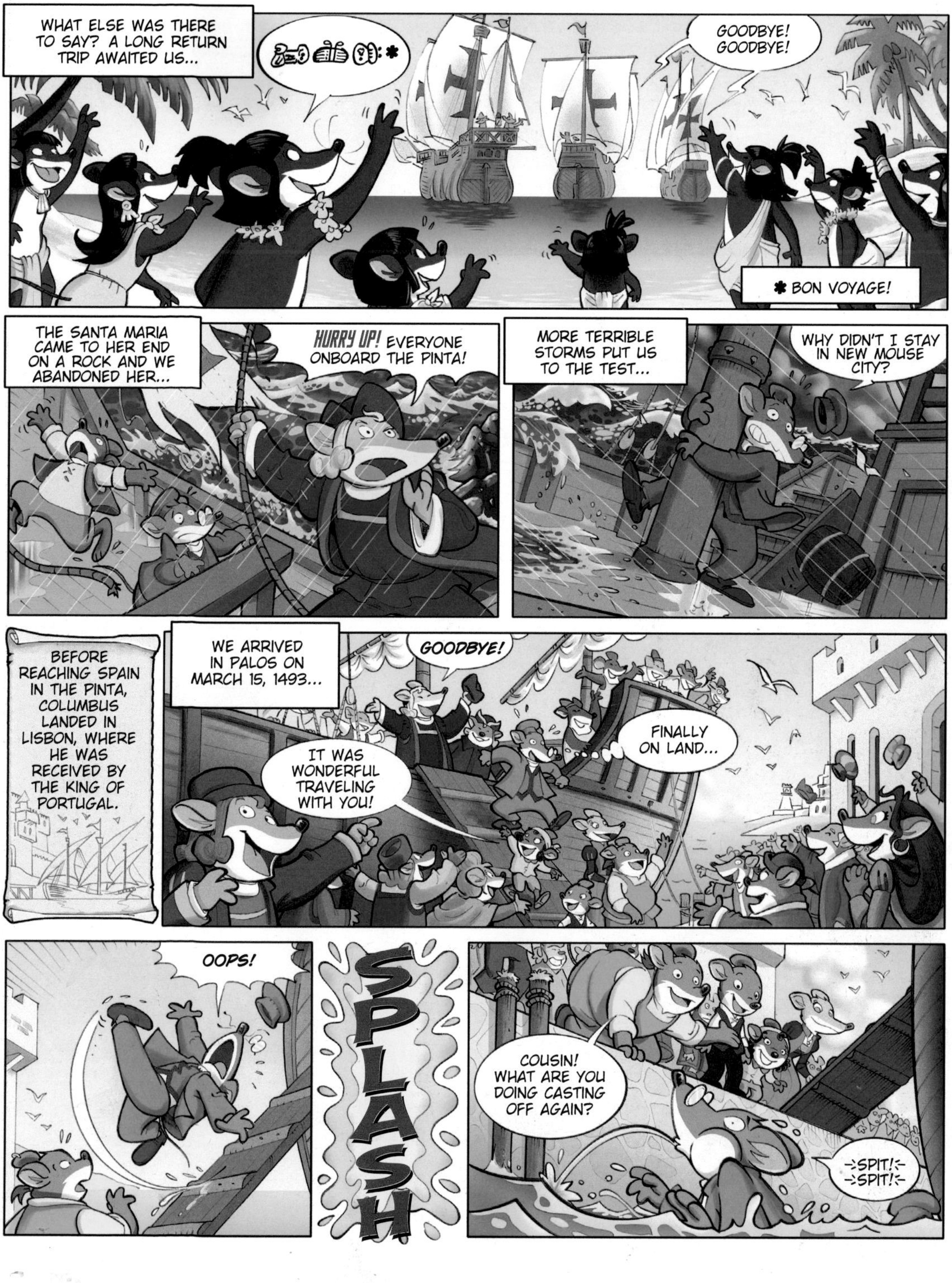

WHAT ELSE WAS THERE TO SAY? A LONG RETURN TRIP AWAITED US...
GOODBYE! GOODBYE!
✽ BON VOYAGE!
THE SANTA MARIA CAME TO HER END ON A ROCK AND WE ABANDONED HER...
HURRY UP! EVERYONE ONBOARD THE PINTA!
MORE TERRIBLE STORMS PUT US TO THE TEST...
WHY DIDN'T I STAY IN NEW MOUSE CITY?
BEFORE REACHING SPAIN IN THE PINTA, COLUMBUS LANDED IN LISBON, WHERE HE WAS RECEIVED BY THE KING OF PORTUGAL.
WE ARRIVED IN PALOS ON MARCH 15, 1493...
GOODBYE!
FINALLY ON LAND...
IT WAS WONDERFUL TRAVELING WITH YOU!
OOPS!
SPLASH
COUSIN! WHAT ARE YOU DOING CASTING OFF AGAIN?
SPIT! SPIT!

AS SOON AS THEY GOT TO LAND, THE PIRATE CATS HOTPAWED IT FROM THE SHIP AND WENT BACK HOME ON THE CATJET...

-PANT!-
-PANT!-

QUICK! LET'S MAKE TRACKS FOR THE CATJET!

MEOWWW! YOU'LL BE HEARING FROM US AGAIN...

MEANWHILE, WE TOOK THE SPEEDRAT BACK TO NEW MOUSE CITY!

FRIENDS! HOW DID IT GO?

MISSION ACCOMPLISHED! WE UNMASKED THE PIRATE CATS AND CHRISTOPHER COLUMBUS DISCOVERED AMERICA!

HURRAH! THOSE SCOUNDRELS DIDN'T CHANGE HISTORY!

BUT LET'S KEEP OUR EYES OPEN FOR THEM! I'M SURE THEY'LL TRY AGAIN!

ARE WE GOING TO TRAVEL BACK IN TIME AGAIN, PROFESSOR?

I REALLY THINK SO!

-SOB!- I HOPE NOT! I'M A VERY QUIET GUY, OR RATHER, A VERY QUIET MOUSE!

AND NOW LET'S CELEBRATE WHAT YOU'VE DONE!

HURRAH! WE UNMASKED THE PIRATE CATS AND SAVED HISTORY!

WOW! CHEESE FOR ALL TASTES!

MY DEAR RODENT FRIENDS, FAREWELL UNTIL THE NEXT ADVENTURE... ANOTHER WHISKERFUL OF AN ADVENTURE WRITTEN BY STILTON, *Geronimo Stilton!*

Watch Out For PAPERCUTZ

Welcome to the first, fact-and-fantasy-filled GERONIMO STILTON graphic novel from Papercutz—the people dedicated to publishing great graphic novels for all ages. And before I forget, allow me to introduce myself—I'm Salicrup, *Jim Salicrup* the Editor-in-Chief of Papercutz. If you've enjoyed Geronimo's profusely illustrated chapter books, then you'll love seeing Geronimo in his graphic novel series! Each graphic novel is like watching an animated Geronimo Stilton movie—except you supply all the voices in your head!

So, while you may be familiar with the Editor-in-Chief of the Rodent's Gazette, you may not be aware of Papercutz. So, here's the story: Papercutz is devoted to publishing the very best graphic novels just for you! Here's a quick rundown on our incredible titles:

CLASSICS ILLUSTRATED and CLASSICS ILLUSTRATED DELUXE -- Two graphic novel series devoted to adapting stories by the World's Greatest Authors into comics!

DANCE CLASS – Fun-filled hijinks with dance students Julie, Alia, and Lucie, by creative team Béka and Crip.

DISNEY FAIRIES – all-new comics starring Tinker Bell and her fairy friends.

ERNEST & REBECCA – The award-winning comics series about the life of a six-and-a-half-year-old girl and her best friend, who is a germ! By Guillaume Bianco, writer, and Antonello Dalena, artist.

GARFIELD & Co – Comics based on the hit Cartoon Network animated series starring the lasagna-loving fat cat, created by Jim Davis.

MONSTER – Featuring the almost normal adventures of an almost ordinary family… and their pet monster. Created by award-winning cartoonist Lewis Trondheim.

NANCY DREW AND THE CLUE CREW – All-new adventures of Carolyn Keene's world-famous girl detective when she was eight years old. Written by Sarh Kinney and Stefan Petrucha, art by Stan Goldberg.

LEGO® NINJAGO -- All-out action with the Masters of Spinjitzu! Written by Greg Farshtey, and illustrated by Paulo Henrique, Paul Lee, and others.

PAPERCUTZ SLICES – Spoofs such as "Harry Potty and the Deathly Boring" and "Hunger Pains" by Stefan Petrucha, writer, and Rick Parker, artist.

POWER RANGERS SUPER SAMURAI – TV's longest-running super-heroes in all-new adventures by Stefan Petrucha, writer, and Paulo Henrique, artist.

SYBIL THE BACKPACK FAIRY – Nina, a young girl, finds a fairy and another magical creature in her backpack. Rodrigue, writer, Dalena & Razzi, artists.

THE THREE STOOGES and THE BEST OF THE THREE STOOGES COMIC-BOOKS – All new stories starring Moe, Larry, and Curly by Stefan Petrucha, Gerorge Gladir, and Jim Salicrup, drawn by Stan Goldberg, and great classic stories by Norman Maurer and Pete Alvarado.

And if that wasn't enough, we're adding new series all the time! To keep up with the latest Papercutz news, be sure to check out www.papercutz.com. And of course, go to www.geroni-mostilton.com for the latest news regarding the time-travelling mouse!

On the following pages, we present a preview of GERONIMO STILTON #2 "The Secret of the Sphinx." And there are plenty more GERONIMO STILTON graphic novels available right now at your favorite booksellers and comicbook stores, and we're busy working on creating even more! We sure hope you'll continue to enjoy GERONIMO STILTON, and even check out our other titles—after all, we're doing it all for you!

Thanks,

JiM

Caricature of Jim by Steve Brodner at the MoCCA Art Fest.

IT ALL BEGAN ON A VERY COLD WINTER MORNING. NEW MOUSE CITY HAD BEEN PARALYZED BY A THREE FOOT BLANKET OF SNOW FOR DAYS...

THE SECRET OF THE SPHINX

...AND I WAS STAYING IN THE COZY WARMTH OF MY HOUSE, FULLY DRESSED, TO KEEP MY **WHISKERS FROM FREEZING!**

BUT HOW CARELESS OF ME! I'VE FORGOTTEN TO INTRODUCE MYSELF: MY NAME IS STILTON, *Geronimo Stilton!* AND I EDIT THE RODENT'S GAZETTE, THE MOST FAMOUSE PAPER ON MOUSE ISLAND!

BRRR!

SO I WAS STAYING IN THE WARMTH WHEN THE DOORBELL RANG!

RIIING

?!?

WHO KNOWS WHO IT COULD BE IN THIS MISERABLE WEATHER...

MOLDY MOZZARELLA! I'M COMING, I'M COMING!

RIIING RIIING

WHO IS IT?

STRANGE -- I DON'T SEE ANYONE, EXCEPT FOR THIS SNOW-MAN...

HMM... MAYBE I DREAMED I HEARD THE DOORBELL!

~SQUEEEAK!~

SSSS

POW

HA, HA, HA... LIKE THE TRICK, COUSIN? COME ON, LET'S HAVE A SNOWBALL FIGHT!

~SIGH~ I SHOULD'VE GUESSED... TRAP!

COME ON, OKAY? I CAN'T PLAY BY MYSELF!

YOU KNOW I DON'T LIKE SNOW VERY MUCH AND WINTER EVEN LESS!

WINTER?

~TSK...~ YOU, MY DEAR GERONIMO, DON'T LIKE ANY SEASON!

"IN SPRING, THERE'S TOO MUCH **WIND**."

"IN SUMMER, IT'S TOO **HOT** AND HUMID."

"IN THE FALL, THERE ARE TOO MANY **LEAVES** ON THE GROUND."

WELL, IF YOU DON'T WANT TO PLAY... YOU CAN ALWAYS OFFER ME A CUP OF HOT CHOCOLATE!

IF THAT'S WHAT YOU WANT, JUST COME INTO THE HOUSE... ~*BRRRRR!*~

VROOOMM

YOO-HOO! CIAO, G! HI, TRAP!

?!?

P-P-PETUNIA?

SKREEE

VROOOMM

HELLO, UNCLE TRAP!

HI, KIDS! ARE YOU GOING SOMEPLACE NICE?

THE SCHOOLS ARE CLOSED, SO I'M TAKING BENJAMIN AND BUGSY WUGSY FOR A RIDE ON MY NEW SNOWMOBILE! I WANTED TO ASK G IF...

SPEAKING OF HIM, WHERE'D HE GO?

GERONIMO? HE WAS HERE JUST A MOMENT AGO!

UH-OH!

RUN INTO THE HOUSE AND LOOK FOR A SHOVEL!

I'LL HELP YOU!

OUR GERONIMO ISN'T HAPPY IF HE'S NOT IN A JAM!

INDEED! HE ALWAYS MANAGES TO GET HIMSELF INTO A FIX!

ATTENTION! ATTENTION! A MESSAGE FOR THE STILTON FAMILY!

HUH?

CALAMITOUS CATS! THAT SNOWMAN TALKS!

I REPEAT, A MESSAGE FOR THE STILTON FAMILY!

HEY! I KNOW THAT *VOICE!*

SQUEAK!

PROFESSOR VON VOLT! IS THAT YOU?

AH, GOOD MORNING, MISS PRETTY PAWS!

55

**Don't miss GERONIMO STILTON
Graphic Novel #2 – "The Secret of the Sphinx"!**

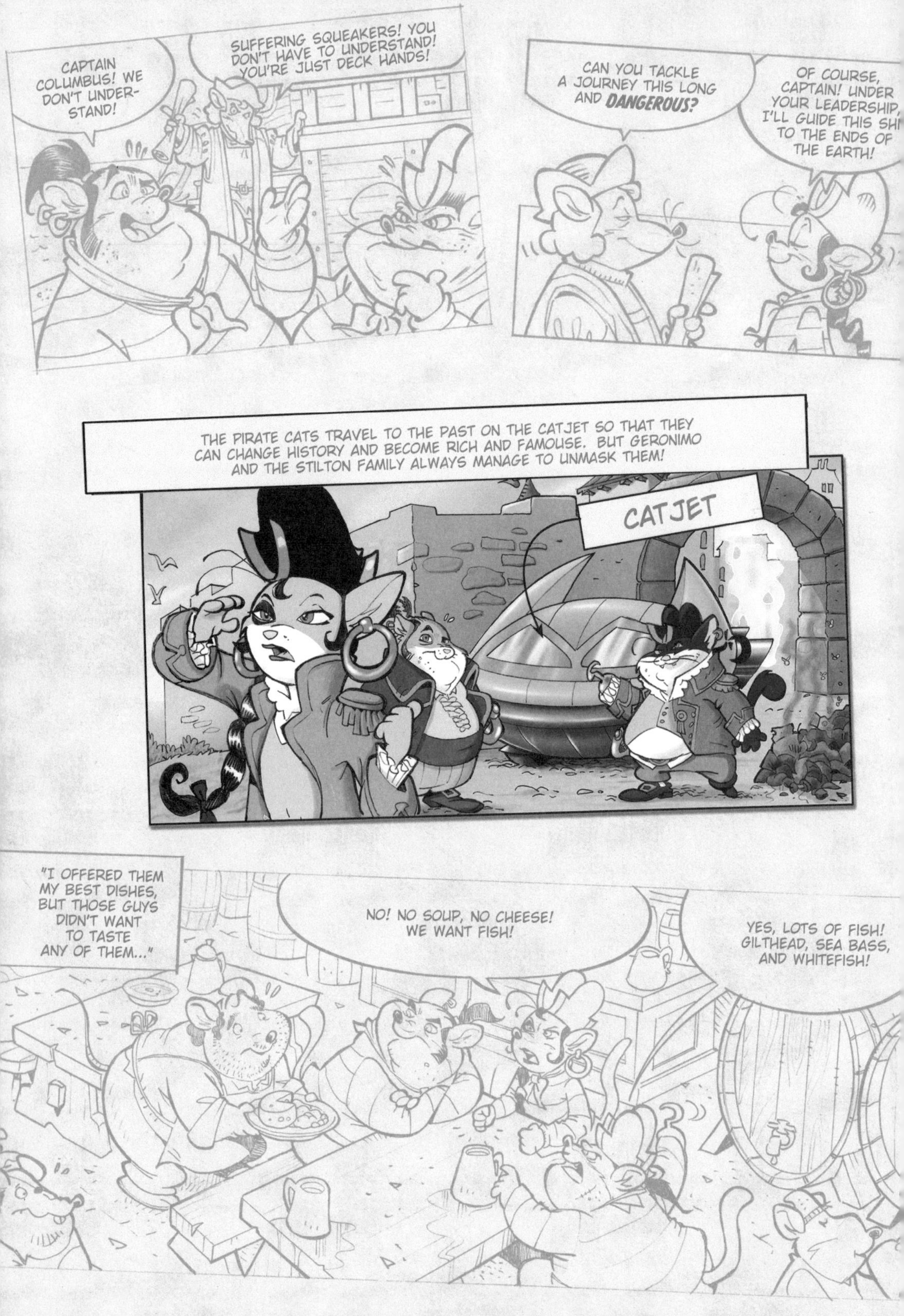
CAPTAIN COLUMBUS! WE DON'T UNDERSTAND!
SUFFERING SQUEAKERS! YOU DON'T HAVE TO UNDERSTAND! YOU'RE JUST DECK HANDS!
CAN YOU TACKLE A JOURNEY THIS LONG AND DANGEROUS?
OF COURSE, CAPTAIN! UNDER YOUR LEADERSHIP, I'LL GUIDE THIS SHI TO THE ENDS OF THE EARTH!
THE PIRATE CATS TRAVEL TO THE PAST ON THE CATJET SO THAT THEY CAN CHANGE HISTORY AND BECOME RICH AND FAMOUSE. BUT GERONIMO AND THE STILTON FAMILY ALWAYS MANAGE TO UNMASK THEM!
CATJET
"I OFFERED THEM MY BEST DISHES, BUT THOSE GUYS DIDN'T WANT TO TASTE ANY OF THEM..."
NO! NO SOUP, NO CHEESE! WE WANT FISH!
YES, LOTS OF FISH! GILTHEAD, SEA BASS, AND WHITEFISH!